Beneath the Dome
by Sam Lucas

ISBN: 978-1-9160640-0-3

BENEATH THE DOME BY SAM LUCAS
© SAM LUCAS 2019, all rights reserved.

www.samlucasbooks.com
e-mail: samlucasbooks@btinternet.com

PUBLISHER - OSCAR PISCINE BOOKS

Image on front cover © SAM LUCAS 2019. No part of this work may be reproduced in part or full without written consent from the author.

Paperback - First edition.

To Brian Cogle

Happy Reading

Sambuca

Tel: 07 8586 246 52

Thank you for buying this book.

Coming soon
'Beyond the Dome'
The sequel to *Beneath the Dome*

ALL PROCEEDS FROM THE SALE OF THIS BOOK GO TO THE ABERDEENSHIRE NORTH FOODBANK

Aberdeenshire North **foodbank**

PLEASE REVIEW THIS BOOK ON AMAZON

Available in Paperback or e-book

FOR OTHER BOOKS IN THIS SERIES, PLEASE GO TO:
WWW.SAMLUCASBOOKS.COM
e-mail: samlucasbooks@btinternet.com

Prologue

Our story begins on the *International Space Station* sometime in the near future, 250 miles above the surface of the planet Earth. Our main protagonists are two Russian cosmonauts called Dmitry Usakov and Yuri Chekov who have been sent to maintain the cameras on board the I.S.S. They are under orders from their commanding officers to speak English at all times to satisfy the terms of the alliance between the various countries that serve on the *Space Station*. This is also to aid any investigations that may occur should an accident happen.

The Earth below is not the one we know, but one that has suffered various hardships over the years: food shortages, plagues, wars and a world wide economic collapse. It is not a dystopian place to live, just different. There are no mobile phones or internet based devices and the technology that is available is more of a status symbol than a necessity with only the wealthiest having access to the latest electronics. Everyone still drives a car, but most are old or aging. Fuel is in short supply and is very expensive.

In the last two decades, America has forged an alliance with China to become a new super power in the world and Britain has made a considerable shift away from America to join forces with Russia to maintain a balance of power. Every nation is very distrustful of one another and everyone's true agenda is a well kept secret. Trust and loyalty are a thing of the past and true friendships are hard to find. If you look close enough, there is an enterprising faction at work and a conspiracy under every stone.

....

In order to enjoy the full effect of this story I would suggest reading it with a Russian accent in your head, this will help with the Pidgin English style the main characters use. But I only suggest using it when the Russian's are speaking.

ACT 1, SCENE 1

Dmitry, a cosmonaut on board the *International Space Station*, appears from behind a curtain and looks out of the window and sees the Earth moving slowly by. He begins to stretch and rotate his arms to shake off a bad nights sleep. Dmitry is in his late 40's and has a solid build with a slight stomach. His hair has gone on top but is silver on the sides and cropped short. His face is on the reddish side and has the tell tale signs of a heavy drinker. He looks back around and Yuri, his fellow cosmonaut on board the I.S.S, enters the small 8ft x 10ft space from the same curtained area he walked in from. Yuri is in his early 40's, he is slim built with a kind vacant face. His hair is dark brown and is slightly curly. His most striking feature is his eyes, they are bright blue and give his face a cheery disposition.

                        DMITRY
How was your first night's sleep on board the *International Space Station* Yuri?

                        YURI
Well, it was...

    (He scratches his hair and wipes his eyes.)

...Like drunken sailor on docks, I did not realise that we would move around so much, especially when we are stationary object in space, but I am glad we have gravity here, and zero gravity is tall tale for masses. How about you?

                    DMITRY
Not too good, I had a late supper with my wife last night and it did not sit well in my stomach. She was going to cook Borsch, but the last beetroot was taken by a little old lady with Jack Russell, so she queued for potatoes and parsnips. She made a dauphinoise out of the potatoes, but I think the milk was off. For pudding she had a surprise for me - Banoffee Pie, except she had no bananas, so guess what she did with the parsnips?...

> *(Dmitry looks around for a drink of water and finds a bottle on the side and takes a sip. Yuri looks on inquisitively and shrugs his shoulders.)*

...She made a PARNOFFEE PIE, I hate parsnips, especially when they are made into a dessert. Parsnips are not a good substitute for bananas...

> *(Dmitry rubs his stomach.)*

...I think it has had a deleterious effect on my well being.

(Dmitry places the water bottle back on the side.)

YURI
Not to worry, I will cook you up a big breakfast, that will settle your stomach. There is nothing better than a nice bowl of porridge with a plate of sausages and eggs, all washed down with some fine black tea.

(Yuri looks through a suitcase to get out his cooking equipment.)

DMITRY
Yuri, what big breakfast, have you forgotten where you are? It's eggs out of a tube for breakfast, we're not at home now.

(Dmitry, looks on at Yuri.)

YURI
I don't intend to eat that space junk, I have brought us some Kolbasa sausages and duck eggs from my local butcher. He's a very nice man, I told him what we were doing and he gave me a big pile of Pirozhki pies for free. Now, where is my burner? I packed it here somewhere along with my mother's favourite frying pan. She only cooks a fry up when you come to visit, so she will not notice it has gone.

(Yuri continues to pull things out of his case and places them on the floor.)

DMITRY

Are you trying to blow us up? You can't light your burner here Yuri; we're in space. The oxygen/hydrogen mix in here is very delicate; didn't you read the manual on space travel by Igo Farinsky? That is essential reading for all good Russian cosmonauts. Where did you think you were going?

YURI

You know, that manual was a bit thick and full of words I had never heard of before, what does apogee and perigee mean? Were they native Indian tribes like the Comanche?...

(Yuri pauses from rifling in the case and looks up at Dmitry.)

...Never-the-less, it was of great help in the end. My kitchen table had a wonky leg for a long time and it was just the right thickness for uneven floor.

(Dmitry raises his right hand and wipes his bald head and becomes animated.)

DMITRY

Don't tell me you didn't read the space

travel training manual. We've got 3 months up here and something might go wrong at anytime. I might have to rely on you for help.

> YURI

Don't worry Dmitry, you are like old mother hen, cluck, cluck...

> *(Yuri removes several items from his case and lays them on the floor.)*

...Ah, here it is, and Rupertvich, I missed you last night, I can't sleep properly without him.

> *(Yuri has finally pulled the frying pan out of the suitcase along with a cuddly toy bear.)*

> DMITRY

Aren't you a little old for bear with tartan trousers? Don't let the Americans or the English see you with that or you will dishonour the both of us as well as the motherland. We will be laughing stock for world to see.

> *(Yuri holds up the bear.)*

> YURI

What are you saying? You must think very little of me Dmitry. I am not simple man with bear; I keep my cigarettes in his belly so my wife can't find them. She is very suspicious of me and is always saying, 'I smell smoke?' I tell her I am burning leaves in back garden, but she has always smart reply.

    (Dmitry takes the bear from Yuri and examines it.)

DMITRY
What does she say?

YURI
She calls me a liar. She says we have no back garden, how can I burn leaves? Then she starts to moan about size of house and starts throwing plates. Before too long she is out in street telling the whole neighbourhood that I am a bad husband who does not provide for her. Then she continues to go on about a prince she once had the chance of marrying and that she married a fool instead...

    (Yuri begins replacing items back in his case.)

...Sometimes, I think I married the wrong woman. Even my father said to me one day when we were out picking blackberries at side of road...

    (Yuri pulls a face and puts on his father's voice.)

...'Yuri, you are marrying the wrong woman, she is too thin. She will moan and complain a lot. Thin people are always moaning and complaining, it is because they are hungry and they cannot relax. Marry a big fat woman, they are slow and don't move around too much; their expectations are small and a good steak pie pleases them. Thin girls want flowers and fine jewellery and to be taken to the ballet.'...

    (Returns to his own voice.)

...But I did not listen, and now I can't even smoke in my own house.

    (Dmitry hands back the bear to Yuri.)

                     DMITRY
Maybe your father is right. You did marry above your station. Ivanka is a beautiful woman who comes from a highly respected family...

    (Dmitry opens a locker door, looks for something, then closes it.)

...It is only normal she would expect the best from her husband...

> (Dmitry opens a small tin, looks at a fishing fly, then puts it back.)

...Such women are not easily satisfied with the simple life.

> (Yuri stares at Dmitry in disbelief.)

YURI
I don't know how you can say such rubbish, I am Russian cosmonaut, who is highly decorated and respected, and comes from a long line of honourable soldiers. My father, and my grandfather, god rest his soul, were both Generals in Russian army...

> (Yuri shakes his left index finger at Dmitry.)

...What was Ivanka, the daughter of a washer woman who came to this country on a cattle boat. Her mother could not even read. When she went to grocery store, where Ivanka's father also worked as a shelf stacker, she could only buy tinned food with pictures on it. Ivanka's background story in magazines was all made up so general population would think she was good match for Russian cosmonaut. She is lucky to have me.

(Yuri takes a cigarette lighter out of the case and closes the lid.)

DMITRY
I am sorry Yuri, I did not know of your situation. What are you doing with that cigarette lighter?

YURI
I am going to have a smoke.

DMITRY
You cannot smoke in here, it is too dangerous, there is nowhere for smoke to go.

(Dmitry moves his hands around to illustrate the smallness of their space, then Yuri points at a vent.)

YURI
Look above you, that grill is taking carbon dioxide and venting it into space, I will smoke underneath it, no one will know.

DMITRY
O.K., but just remember I told you it is not a good idea; everyone will smell it and there will be trouble. Whatever you do, do not let the English see, they will want to trade used teabags or stale

biscuits for one of your cigarettes. I am going to check on camera no. 6, I will be back in five minutes.

                    YURI
I will put the radio on while you are gone.

    (Dmitry leaves their quarters through a door leading out into the corridor and Yuri walks towards a radio and begins to tune in a station. A song starts to play.)

Scene fades.

ACT 1, SCENE 2

Yuri is looking out at Earth through a large porthole and smoking a cigarette. Their quarters are looking more homely with added items carefully placed in suitable locations: a coffee machine, some candles, a gas burner with pans, board games, books, a wall clock, plastic flowers, a vegetable rack with vegetables, two glasses and a pile of paper napkins, a condiment set with various mustards and sauces and a small reading lamp. Dmitry walks into the room carrying a green box under his left arm.

                    DMITRY
I see you've been busy. It is good to see we are still alive and that you did not cause fire...

   *(Dmitry looks around their
   quarters for a minute to absorb
   all the changes. He places his
   green box on the side.)*

...Camera no.6 needs a new card, Earth is looking a little skewed. Where are the elliptical cards Yuri?

(Yuri turns from the window and looks at Dmitry.)

YURI

What elliptical cards?

DMITRY

You know, the black cards with light blue edge?

(Yuri pulls out his suitcase and starts to unpack everything.)

YURI

I did see them before the launch, but I had to make room in my suitcase for a packet of Kasha and some herbs and spices, so I took them out to repack everything. I must have forgotten to put them back in.

(Dmitry puts his hands in the air.)

DMITRY

Yuri, you are imbecile, what are we going to do now? We must change that card before it deteriorates any further and exposes truth about planet.

YURI

I am sorry Dmitry, but if truth comes out, maybe we will be heroes.

DMITRY
If truth comes out we will be shot and our families will be sent to prison.

YURI
Maybe we could close camera down, repair card, and put it back, it would only be off for a few hours.

DMITRY
What would we tell *Mission Control*, it is only supposed to be off for 45 minutes, there is already growing suspicion about planet's shape in world's media.

YURI
We will tell them the camera was faulty and repairs were needed, simple.

DMITRY
I hope for both our sakes we pull this off, if the people of Earth discover world is flat like pancake, there will be trouble. It will only be a matter of time before they find out about Dome and then the fan will be covered in big mess.

(Dmitry is looking slightly agitated and is starting to sweat.)

YURI
Everything will be fine, we will just have to tell a few lies. People on Earth

believe what we tell them, they are all gullible.

                    DMITRY
Put away that suitcase, all you have done is annoy me with that suitcase since I got up this morning. Get your space suit on, we are going outside.

                    YURI
Dmitry, you are not looking well, you are sweating and you look troubled...

> *(Yuri closes the suitcase and pushes it out of the way. Dmitry is now sweating profusely and is wringing his hands.)*

...Shall I leave radio on?

                    DMITRY
Yes, turn it up, everyone will think we are still here eating breakfast.

                    YURI
Did you say outside?

                    DMITRY
Yes, why? It is just like simulation without water.

                    YURI
I can't do it, my space suit won't take

pressure.

DMITRY
What do you mean, these suits are made by finest tailors and technicians in all of Russia.

YURI
Maybe so, but my mother thought she knew better.

DMITRY
What are you saying?

YURI
Do you remember night out at Forte Music Club when waitress dress came off on chair leg?

DMITRY
How could I forget a night like that, not only did you embarrass that poor girl, but you set fire to your shirt with cigarette. But what has that got to do with your mother and your space suit?

YURI
Well, that night my mother stay at home and watch our French Poodle, Gertrud. To pass time, she read magazine about great cosmonauts of our generation. She found a picture of me and thought the suit made me look fat, so she took personal life support system out to make it look less

bulky. Now it is just a mechanics boiler suit, not space suit; but fit is very comfortable and I look good.

                    DMITRY
Yuri, you are like appendix, something you have throughout life but don't understand why. What did you think you were coming here to do, take photos for album and keep me company while I do all the work?...

> *(Dmitry reaches into a locker and pulls out a space suit. Yuri takes a cigarette from his bear.)*

...Well not to worry, I have spare suit you can borrow. Now, put down tartan bear and get dressed.

Scene fades.

ACT 1, SCENE 3

Outside the International Space Station, Yuri and Dmitry are making their way to camera 6 to replace the elliptical card. Their movements are slow and awkward in their space suits and they look clumsy and ill at ease. Below, the Earth rotates slowly by, it is flat, but round.

YURI
I don't like this, these goldfish bowl helmets are too tight and I forgot to wear my glasses.

DMITRY
I have never seen you with glasses; you passed eye exam just like me.

YURI
I memorised eye chart to pass exam, I can see things close up, but you are just a blur.

DMITRY
Yuri, I am only 6 feet away, how did you manage EVAC simulation on Earth?

(Yuri is holding on tight to anything he can feel and is moving slowly.)

YURI

I usually wear contact lenses, but I forgot to bring them, I was too excited about mission and free food from butcher. I am sorry Dmitry, but I can still hold screws and card for you while you work; that will free up a hand for you. I can also keep an eye out for meteor showers.

DMITRY

How can you see meteor shower if you can't even see me? Yuri, you are a real melon head, I think you only join Space Programme because you couldn't get real job.

YURI

No, I wanted to know truth about cosmos and witness beauty of space, but I did not think it would ever happen, but fate stepped in and dealt me a new hand.

(Dmitry is now unscrewing some bolts with an electric gun.)

DMITRY

How did you get into Space Programme? Did you pull some strings and sit next to the right person in sauna at golf club?

YURI
No, it was nothing like that.

(Yuri moves closer to Dmitry and is ready to hold the bolts.)

DMITRY
Then what?

YURI
Well, if you are pushing the subject, I will tell you. On a cold September morning a man came to my parent's house and told me that if I did not have his money by next Thursday, he would break my knee caps and burn house down. This was not a good start to my day, so I sat down and thought for a while. I knew I would not have money and went to train station to leave for new city; I could only hope he would leave my parents alone. On train, I shared a compartment with a nice man also called Yuri, who was on his way to start cosmonaut training at Moscow Space Academy. I, on the other hand, was on the run from loan shark and had not worked for 2 years and only had 10 Rubles to my name.

DMITRY
Yuri, what are you saying, you are not you? Did you kill someone? I was already feeling nauseous before space walk, but now I feel sick, not in a motion sickness way, but in a fat boy who eat too much

cake on his birthday kind of way.

YURI
Dmitry, don't worry, I did not kill anyone. Man choke on fish bone in dining car on train. The porter tried to save him, but it was too late. I had had an interesting afternoon with the other Yuri, and he told me of his plans. So, I take entrance papers to academy from corpse and stuff in pocket. Our last names were very similar, Chekov and Schekov. So I tell people at academy it is just an administration error and lady at reception alter paperwork and I'm in. At home, I tell my parents I have entered Space Programme as a special case for the deprived and everything is peachy. The other Yuri had already done entrance exam, and had passed all mathematics and physics tests with flying colours, so I only had to do the simulation training with you.

(Dmitry now has the card in his hands and is ready to return to the Space Station.)

DMITRY
But what about all the onboard navigation and flight control systems! How did you know what buttons to press?

YURI
Back up team always enter simulation first, so I watch what buttons they

pressed and made notes. If anything became too difficult, I would look busy and ask you to get that for me. I just bluffed my way through, if people think you are genius, then you are.

                    DMITRY
What happened about loan shark, did he not turn up at your house and threaten your parents?

                    YURI
That was other piece of good fortune. Ambulance that rush to save other Yuri on train, hit another car in traffic accident...

    (Yuri starts to laugh.)

...Turned out to be loan shark with friends on way to parents house. The car blew up on impact with ambulance. Unfortunately for them, boot of car was full of cans of petroleum and Molotov cocktails. They were all burnt to a crisp.

    (Yuri is still chuckling.)

                    DMITRY
Why are you laughing, what about poor ambulance driver, did he die also?

                    YURI
Sadly yes, but not from accident. He

suffered a major heart attack while driving and crossed over on to other side of road and, well, instant death - bang! They all go up like bomb...

(Yuri is still smiling.)

...Very lucky day for me, but not so lucky for others. I don't know about you but I am getting hungry, how much longer will you be?

DMITRY
That is it, we can go back inside now. How can you be hungry after a confession like that?

YURI
I have nothing to be ashamed of, I might not have entered the academy with clean hands, but I have done nothing wrong. Besides, I look more like cosmonaut than you do. If you were in a line up with 9 other people and I was asked, who do you think is Russian cosmonaut? I would not pick you, you look more like a farmer than famous Spaceman. I would give you tractor over rocket ship, all that is missing is piece of straw from mouth.

DMITRY
If I were not in space suit right now, I would sock you in face. I have known you for many years and considered you close friend, but today, I don't know who you

are.   Is it joke Yuri?

                    YURI
I am sorry Dmitry, it is no joke, maybe it is a bit much for you to take in. Perhaps I should have told you before now, but I thought you might say something to someone and I not go on mission, this way you have three months to think about it.

                    DMITRY
We will talk about it later, how long have we been outside?

                    YURI
One hour and twenty-four minutes.

                    DMITRY
You return to *Station*, I will finish off here and be with you shortly.

                    YURI
O.K., I will make some soup and feed Boris.

     *(Yuri's words drift off into space
     and are not heard clearly.)*

                    DMITRY
...And stay away from the Americans and the English.

Scene fades.

ACT 1, SCENE 4

Yuri is back inside the Space Station and is making soup over a small gas burner. He has chopped up various vegetables and is now placing them into a saucepan along with some fish. Shortly afterwards, Dmitry returns holding a black elliptical card with a blue highlighted edge.

                    DMITRY
That soup smells good, what is it?

                    YURI
Fish soup. My grandmother's recipe: salmon fillets, big eye ocean perch, potatoes, onions, parsley, carrots, black pepper and a little dill to serve. It is coming on very nicely, even if I do say so myself. Now, where is salt?...

   (Yuri looks around for the salt.)

...Ah yes, here it is. Dmitry, will you pass me container marked bio-hazardous material.

                    DMITRY
Why are you using these containers, they are for space organisms and harmful materials.

                    YURI
I knew most people would not look inside
container marked bio-hazard, so I hid all
of my condiments inside.

   (Dmitry looks down at Yuri.)

                    DMITRY
I have just realised, you have burner
going, what did I tell you.

                    YURI
Don't worry, everything is fine, and the
soup is nearly ready. Hand me some bowls
and we will eat.

   *(Dmitry takes two bowls from a
   shelf and hands them to Yuri.)*

                    DMITRY
I was thinking outside about your story...

   *(Dmitry picks up the elliptical
   card and places it on the side.)*

...You may have got into academy under
false pretences, but you did pass rest of
exams by yourself. You might not be the
best mathematician in world and your
physics is at primary school level at
best, but who cares?...

   *(Dmitry walks over to smell the
   soup.)*

...Space Programme is big lie. What are we doing here anyway, pinning black card to camera to hide truth about planet. We have already sold ourselves out! If everyone below knew about Dome and the Overseers, there would be anarchy and our necks would be first ones for chop.

YURI

I am glad you have forgiven me. Here, try some soup.

(Yuri holds out a spoon full of soup for Dmitry to try.)

DMITRY

Yuri, this is the best. Such flavour. Maybe I was a little hasty when I told you not to use burner. The dill is so fragrant and adds a wonderful high note to soups solid foundation. Certainly beats those tubes of powdered egg. Tell me Yuri, what is secret to good soup? When Olga makes traditional Russian soup it does not taste like this, more like rubber plimsoll I wear to primary school.

YURI

My secret is simple. Just use fresh local produce that is in season, farmed using sustainable methods and grown organically, add some love and stir. Maybe your wife is not good cook, perhaps you should get some help when we return. Tell your wife that you are going to be very busy at work and she will have to take on more responsibilities away from home, and to alleviate her chores, you will hire a maid and a cook for her.

                    DMITRY
Yuri, that is a great idea. Truth be told, my wife is terrible cook. She once tried to make *Chicken Kiev* with tin of spam and stale loaf. It is very difficult to get right ingredients these days with food shortages getting worse. She did not want to disappoint me so she took only thing left on shelf and tried to do the best she could. She had queued in line for two hours at local shop for fresh chicken, but man in wheelchair buy last chicken on shelf. I tell her she must get to shop at 6am in morning to get best stuff, but she does not listen. Even so, that is not real problem. Her brain is prone to flights of fancy and pan of water on stove for boiling egg is dry before egg hits pan.

     (Dmitry and Yuri sit down at the
     table and begin to eat.)

                    YURI
Would you like some bread with your soup, Dmitry?

(Dmitry is eating his soup with the stomach of a hungry man.)

DMITRY
Where have you got bread?

YURI
In cupboard behind you marked diagnostic tools.

DMITRY
Yuri, that is a lovely looking Brioche, but where are tools?

YURI
Don't worry, they have been put in box under bed, they can go back when we have eaten loaf in 2 days time.

DMITRY
O.K., but don't forget.

YURI
Now, I must feed Boris.

(Dmitry breaks off a piece of bread and dips it in his soup, then looks up at Yuri.)

DMITRY
Who is Boris? You mentioned him before but I thought I misheard.

YURI
Boris is pet mouse.

DMITRY
Yuri, pet mouse! You are kidding, you did not bring a mouse up here?

YURI
It is alright, he is in container for spare Petri dishes and eye droppers, he cannot escape.

DMITRY
Yuri, that mouse is danger to everyone on *Space Station*. It might come in contact with some unknown space virus and turn us all into mutants.

YURI
Dmitry, you are starting to believe propaganda that government print in scary pamphlet they hand out each year to lower class population. What is it called again?

DMITRY
'How to keep your family safe from infectious diseases.'

YURI
That is it, how did you remember name?

(Dmitry finishes his soup and places the bowl on the table.)

DMITRY

In my younger days I was a pamphleteer for the government promoting health supplement GSM124B. I believed it was a good thing for community to take food supplement and to be informed about contagious viruses and diseases. I did not realise it was form of control to keep masses from city centres. It is hard to believe that I fell for all that crap. Imagine informing people that contact with others was dangerous and could spread plague. All because the rich did not want the poor in the cities. It all started when they handed out that stupid mint flavoured protein bar - *'Green Soya'*; who knew it was drug? That was terrible time for the motherland, death was common occurrence in deprived areas. Even now many are still addicted.

YURI

I remember lots of death and people jumping off of tall building after they had eaten that supplement. Where I lived they called it the *Superman Bar*. I came from deprived area and saw many things. My brother caught ketchup plague; he was not a pretty sight. Every day he would wait outside MacDonald's for rubbish to be thrown. He would then go through bags for ketchup sachet, just to squeeze last drop. When he returned home we all knew where he had been. His lips were bright red and his white shirt was all stained with tomato smudges. My mother told him he would die from activity but he did not listen.

(Yuri picks up tartan bear and takes out a cigarette.)

DMITRY
Did he die from plague?

YURI
No, lid of bin fell on his head and he forgot who he was, and he wondered off. We searched for him for two weeks without trace and then I find him sleeping outside florist shop. He did not know who I was and ran away. I try to chase him, but before I could catch him he ran in front of bus. Driver could not believe the amount of blood in Street...

(Yuri places the cigarette into his mouth, lights it and takes a drag.)

...but then we find hundreds of tomato sachets stuffed in shirt.

DMITRY
I am very sorry Yuri, I did not know you

had lost your brother, it must have been terrible for your family, especially for your mother.

             YURI
It was, she had an awful problem getting stain out of shirt.

             DMITRY
What? I mean losing a son must be dreadful?

             YURI
Dmitry, he did not die. After bus hit him, he remember who he was and came home with me. He now works in travel agent selling holiday coach tours to Ukraine. I am glad to say he beat his addiction, but tomato sauce can be terrible for some people, they will put it on everything.

             DMITRY
Yuri, sometimes, I feel exhausted after conversation with you and I feel I have learnt nothing, other times, like today, I feel like man with pet monkey.

       (*Yuri collects the soup bowls and
       makes his way behind the curtain.
       He is heard banging crockery
       around in a sink.*)

             YURI
Boris, has escaped?

DMITRY
What?

(Yuri walks back into their main living quarters with an empty container in his hands.)

YURI
Boris has escaped, he must have climbed out of container.

(Dmitry rises to his feet to examine the container.)

DMITRY
How did he push lid off?

YURI
I did not put lid on, I thought he would not be able to breathe.

DMITRY
You could have put holes in lid.

YURI
I did not think of that. Dmitry, what shall we do?

DMITRY
Not bring mouse on *Space Station* in first place.

YURI
Dmitry, it is too late for sarcasm, Boris

will be scared, he is all alone on strange ship.

DMITRY
You worry about mouse, if the American finds him first, we will be in serious trouble. Did you bring any cheese?

YURI
Yes, it is in compartment marked experimental prototypes, behind metal orb wrapped in tin foil.

(Dmitry rifles through a locker and pulls out a round cheese.)

DMITRY
Yuri, this is finest French Camembert! Where did you get this? I have not seen this since my sister had her braces removed and we went for treat in local café to eat crusty roll with soft cheese.

(Dmitry takes the cheese out of the wrapper, smells it and begins to eat it.)

YURI
Dmitry, I see him, pass cheese. Dmitry what are you doing?

DMITRY
Delicious, mmm, it is so good.

YURI
What are you doing? He is right there; give me cheese.

DMITRY
I am sorry, this is too good for mouse, here is wrapper; that will have to do.

YURI
I will place in container and he will go in himself, he loves Camembert cheese. See now, watch...

> (Boris, the mouse, jumps into the container and starts sniffing the cheese wrapper.)

...Look Dmitry, see I told you.

DMITRY
Quickly put on lid...

> (Dmitry wipes his mouth with a paper napkin.)

...That is an unusual looking mouse and quite fat, what is it?

YURI
He is a Dutch mouse, looks like small Panda; white with two black eyes...

> (Yuri quickly places a lid on the container.)

...Got him, but I must put hole in lid.

> (Crackling and static start to come from the radio.)

                    VLADIMIR
This is *R.K.A Mission Control* calling *International Space Station*, come in, over.

                    DMITRY
Yuri, stay calm, it is only daily check, put that mouse somewhere safe...

> (Dmitry picks up the radio hand set.)

...This is Dmitry Usakov calling *R.K.A Mission Control*, over.

                    VLADIMIR
Where have you guys been? We have been trying to contact you for the past 2 hours.

                    DMITRY
Sorry, we had to carry out emergency repair work on elliptical card for camera 6, but we ran into complications and we had to shut it down.

                    VLADIMIR
Why did we lose communications?

DMITRY
Damage to console, err, circuit board had a minor burnout, but it is fixed now.

VLADIMIR
Funny, we weren't reading a malfunction down here. Well O.K., when you have a chance, can you send down a status report?

DMITRY
Will do, over.

YURI
Good thinking Dmitry, now everything is peachy. I don't know about you but I could use a sleep, all this excitement has made me tired.

DMITRY
You have only been up three hours, the shift is not finished for another five.

YURI
Five hours, impossible! I cannot keep my eyes open, I will need at least a nap until lunch time. It must be this fake air making me tired and the constant revolution of the Earth below. It is very relaxing watching it gently roll by with great balls of cotton covering its surface. Now I must go.

DMITRY
I suppose a little sleep would not hurt,

but we must be awake when *Mission Control* contacts us later.

                    YURI
O.K., see you in a while.

    (Dmitry and Yuri disappear behind a curtain.)

Scene fades.

ACT 2, SCENE 1

After a few hours sleep, Yuri is awoken by an alarm. He moves quickly when he sees smoke coming from a console in the main cabin.

　　　　　　　　YURI
Dmitry, wake up! Something is wrong, there is smoke coming from behind computer console.

　　(Yuri gets out of bed and tries to wake Dmitry.)

　　　　　　　　DMITRY
I never said you were fat, I said you were ugly.

　　　　　　　　YURI
Dmitry, wake up!

　　(Yuri starts to shake Dmitry.)

　　　　　　　　DMITRY
I have given you blanket... What? What is it? Where is Mamma? Yuri, why are you here? What's that noise? Yuri, what's happened?

　　　　　　　　YURI
Fire, Dmitry. Quick!

(Dmitry jumps out of bed and goes towards the fire.)

VLADIMIR
Come in *Space Station*, we have warning lights saying you have a fire. Dmitry, Yuri, come in over.

DMITRY
Yuri, quick! Pull that cover off the console, I will get extinguisher.

VLADIMIR
Space Station come in, over.

(Yuri manages to pull the cover off the console.)

YURI
That is it. Dmitry, put out fire!

(Dmitry starts to read instructions on the fire extinguisher.)

DMITRY
Pull tag and remove pin, hold at base of fire and squeeze trigger.

YURI
Dmitry, what are you doing?

DMITRY
O.K., I have it!

(Dmitry uses the fire extinguisher and puts the fire out. Smoke fills the room and Yuri opens the door to the corridor. He waves a tea towel around to dissipate the smoke.)

YURI
Well done, it's out! Looks a real mess, all chewed up.

VLADIMIR
Space Station, come in, over!

DMITRY
Yuri, get that.

(Yuri goes to the radio and picks up the hand set.)

YURI
Mission Control, this is *Space Station*, Yuri speaking.

VLADIMIR
What's going on up there?

YURI
Dmitry, kill that alarm, I can't hear myself think. Control... Small fire, but under control now, Dmitry has put it out.

VLADIMIR
What started the fire?

YURI
Looks like faulty wiring behind console 7, it looks like it's been chewed by mouse.

VLADIMIR
Chewed by a mouse?

YURI
Err, no, looks like wiring in old house, when was this stuff last checked, looks rotten. What do you think Dmitry?

  (Yuri hands Dmitry the radio hand
  set.)

DMITRY
Looks like old wiring to me. Ha, old fuse box, it was bound to happen. Lucky we were here, this whole place might have gone up in smoke.

  (Dmitry hands back the hand set to
  Yuri.)

YURI
Dmitry is right, if we had not been on shift, we may have died in our sleep.

VLADIMIR
Can't understand it, that console should have been replaced two months ago with new

equipment.

   (Yuri switches the radio to the speaker microphone.)

                   DMITRY
Maybe someone has been lacking in their duties. Well never mind, no one was hurt. We will fix it.

                  VLADIMIR
We're about to lose contact for 20 minutes, over.

                   DMITRY
Understood, over.

                    YURI
Dmitry, look! Here comes Hank, the American.

   (Hank, an American astronaut also on board the I.S.S. enters their quarters. Hank is 6ft 4 inches tall and comes from Oklahoma. He has a dark complexion and a muscular build.)

                    HANK
Say, what the heck is going on here? What have you guys gotten us into?

                    YURI
Nothing to worry about, just a small fire.

HANK
A fire! How did that start?

YURI
Just some faulty wiring, but it is alright. Dmitry has saved us all from catastrophe, he is hero. With no regard for himself, he quickly put out fire and had situation under control. You, along with the English, owe Dmitry your life. In motherland we would celebrate for a week. We would sing songs, drink vodka and pay tribute to his greatness. We would even erect big statue in his honour if planning permission was permitted.

> (Yuri quickly covers the console with a blanket to hide the mess, while Hank tries to get a closer look.)

HANK
Well, we appreciate your cool head Dmitry, if you say everything is fine, I'll be getting back to my duties.

> (Hank takes one last look around and leaves.)

YURI
O.K., well thanks for popping by.

DMITRY
Yuri, where is mouse?

YURI
In box.

DMITRY
Did you put the lid on this time?

YURI
Yes, I even cut hole for lid...

(Yuri walks over to Boris' container.)

...Look Dmitry, mouse has gone!

DMITRY
Yuri, I told you to make holes in lid, you have big flap.

YURI
Well, I did not want him to suffocate, he has little lungs. I am worried Dmitry, he will be scared, poor little fellow.

DMITRY
Scared, he is making a home for himself. Just look at that console, it's ruined. Yuri this is your fault, you do not think before you act. If that mouse gets into the main computer we will be in serious trouble.

YURI
Don't worry, I will put cheese out for him and he will come home to his papa.

                    DMITRY
Help me tidy this mess up, we will fix
this console and then make a report to
Mission Control.

                    YURI
O.K., but I must use little boys room
first.

                    DMITRY
Alright, but be quick.

Scene fades.

ACT 2, SCENE 2

A few hours have passed without incident, The cabin is looking tidy again and Yuri is cooking sausages over a naked flame. Dmitry is reading a book on fly fishing and humming to himself.

                    YURI
Dmitry?

                    DMITRY
Yes, what is it?

                    YURI
I have question about *Space Station*...

    (Dmitry puts his book down and looks at Yuri.)

...I was reading about orbits and I did not understand how *Space Station* stays in one place and does not fall down to Earth.

                    DMITRY
Since you did not bother to read manual, I will tell you. We hang from Dome by five big metal cables. In the middle of the cable is a rubber section to prevent transference of power and electrocution. Look out of window, you will see cable, but notice that the camera is always aimed at Earth and can't see it.

(Yuri moves from the burner with a sausage on a fork and looks out the window.)

YURI
Yes, I can see it...

(Yuri looks back at Dmitry.)

...But who made the Dome and what does it do?

DMITRY
The Overseers made the Dome to keep us trapped on Earth, the academy must have told you all about the Overseers before you got on mission.

YURI
The academy had many classes, but my mother needed help at home with her chicken deliveries, so I skipped a few lessons to help her out. She was a frail old woman even back then, and the truck she drove was too big for her to handle, so I drove sometimes when her orders were behind.

DMITRY
I did not know your mother drove a truck, what firm did she work for?

(Yuri walks back to the stove and begins heating his sausage again.)

YURI
No firm, she was an independent retailer.

DMITRY
Where did she get chicken from?

YURI
I am not sure, I never asked her.

DMITRY
You know, my father was in the chicken business as well.

YURI
No, I did not know that, funny us both having parents in the poultry business.

(Yuri hands over the cooked sausage to Dmitry and starts to cook one for himself.)

DMITRY
It is interesting that your mother delivered chicken at the same time you were at academy.

(Dmitry waves his sausage around.)

YURI
Why is that interesting, you were telling me about Overseers and Dome.

DMITRY
It is interesting because shipment of chickens disappeared every week from warehouse at my father's business, but we never catch thief. My father was convinced it was someone local and somebody we must know.

YURI
Why all this interest in chickens from over 15 years ago. You can't think my mother stole chickens from your father's warehouse? She was always old and frail, even when she was a young girl she walked with glass cane and had a *Strongboy* in house to open lemonade bottle. It would not be the sort of caper my mother would get involved with, she maybe would run numbers now again for a little old Italian guy who owned a Pizzeria, but heavy lifting was not her thing. She did not even like carrier bags because they had handles and that meant a form of exertion, even if bag was empty. I am sorry Dmitry, I would like to help you out with your historic crime riddle, but I cannot shed any light on the disappearance of a few old chickens. Now tell me about Overseers.

DMITRY
O.K., if you say so, but it is interesting, that is all I am saying.

YURI
Dmitry, it is not interesting, it is just coincidence, that is all, now please, tell me about Overseers and Dome.

DMITRY
Very well, but first pass me another sausage, they are extra tasty, where did you get them from?

YURI
I did not steal them, if that is what you are thinking. My mother got them for me from local vicar. He keeps pigs and every year he has them killed for freezer. My mother sometimes places bet on horse for him. Before we left he had good fortune, so when mother go to settle up winnings, the vicar give her a pound of sausages as a thank you, she then gave them to me for trip.

DMITRY
Yuri, I am sorry I brought up this whole chicken affair, I will tell you about Overseers.

YURI
Good.

(Dmitry adjusts his seat.)

DMITRY
Please understand what I am going to tell

you is only known by a few governmental bodies and that the information is still top secret.

(Yuri looks at Dmitry.)

YURI
Don't worry Dmitry, I am good at keeping secret. It has taken you fifteen years to learn that I am imposter.

DMITRY
Yes, well, I am trying to forget that.

YURI
C'mon, spill the beans?

DMITRY
Very well. Make yourself comfortable...

(Yuri sits back in his chair and begins to smoke. Dmitry moves his green box from his chair and sits down.)

...The Overseers were an alien race of people that came to Earth five thousand years ago when our planet was sparsely populated. They landed in a place known as Mesopotamia where the Sumerians lived. This is where they made first contact.

YURI
Mesopotamia? I have never heard of this place!

DMITRY
It's known as Southern Iraq today.

YURI
The Middle East? It must have been hot for them. I hope they brought a good sun block, it is easy to get sunburn without adequate protection. Did they have delicate skin? Was it very bright for them? What did they look like Dmitry?

DMITRY
If you shut up for a minute, I will tell you.

YURI
Sorry, I am eager to learn.

DMITRY
They looked like us, but their heads were elongated and their skin was tough and grey like elephant.

YURI
No need for sun block then, elephants are used to sun.

DMITRY
Yes, they are...

>   *(Dmitry raises his eyebrows and*
>   *takes the last bite from his*
>   *sausage.)*

...Those sausages are very nice, do you have any more?

                    YURI

Yes, here...

>   *(Yuri hands Dmitry another*
>   *sausage.)*

...tell me more about the Overseers Dmitry.

                    DMITRY

When the Overseers found Earth, they sent many scout ships down to the surface to survey planet. After a few days, the survey teams became sick and grew weak. They had all been infected by an unknown virus. You see Yuri, the Overseers had no knowledge of sickness, they had never been ill before and they didn't die.

                    YURI

Are you saying they were immortal?

                    DMITRY

That is what the ancient scrolls say.

                    YURI

Sounds like a good deal...

(Yuri puffs on his cigarette.)

...But if they were married to my wife, long life would seem more of a curse than a blessing. So, what happened next?

DMITRY
To stop spread of disease getting to mother ship, the Overseers left their survey teams behind to die on Earth. To protect universe, they placed a big Dome around planet. So, for last five thousand years, Earth has been in quarantine...

YURI
Quarantine? Why would they do that?

DMITRY
The Overseers probably thought at some point we would develop space flight and travel amongst the stars. Putting a force field around Earth would stop us infecting other worlds. Death is not normal Yuri, it is a disease. To rest of universe, Earth is plague.

YURI
Dmitry, this is heavy, I need another cigarette, it is a lot to take in. So Earth is cancer in universe? I can see why we would keep this a secret, but dying is natural part of life. What do other planets do about population growth, they

would become crowded over time.

DMITRY
Ancient Sumerian scrolls tell only part of story, Yuri. Much of our history is lost.

YURI
I think we are lucky really, if they had survived on our planet it would be too full by now and we would be bow to their fiddle. Death is good thing, it protects us from rest of universe...

(Yuri rubs his chin.)

...Y'know Dmitry, this is a blessing, not a curse. I am sure by now, some alien species would have come to Earth and taken it for themselves. The Overseers wanted it 5000 years ago, but it backfired on them.

DMITRY
Yuri, are you not forgetting one small thing?

(Dmitry walks over to the window and looks at Earth.)

YURI
What?

DMITRY
We die. It takes the fun out of life...

> (Dmitry looks back from the window and faces Yuri.)

...Just think of it Yuri, immortality. It is what everyone strives for, the chance to live forever...

> (Dmitry becomes animated and starts to gesticulate.)

...Think of all the things you could accomplish with a life that does not have time clock.

YURI

It does seem like something that might be appealing...

> (Yuri takes out a cigarette and lights it.)

...but life can be tedious, an endless stream of repetition - sleep, wash, eat, work, eat, wash, sleep. A time limit to life makes us creative and become involved in the now, if you live forever, there is always tomorrow. Procrastination could last for decades, people would become lazy and see no need to do anything today when there is endless supply of tomorrows...

> (He takes a long drag on his cigarette.)

...I think we are a reminder to rest of universe that life should not be taken for granted, that it is precious. It is only when a loved one has passed that we truly understand their worth, because in life we took it all for granted...

(Yuri stubs out his cigarette. Dmitry looks on thoughtfully.)

...Death has very important job in life, it makes us take action today and keeps us motivated.

DMITRY
You make a good argument Yuri. You are smarter than you look and on rare occasions you even make sense.

Scene fades.

ACT 2, SCENE 3

A couple of hours have passed and there is still no sign of Boris. Yuri has been looking over the *Space Station* for him, but after an extensive search into various nooks and crannies he returns empty handed to his quarters. Dmitry is fast asleep in his chair and has spent the last two hours tinkering inside his green box. The lid is slightly open and exposes some fishing flies. Dmitry begins to stir when he hears Yuri enter their cabin and quickly closes the lid to his green box, but not before Yuri sees the contents inside.

                    DMITRY
You are back, any luck with Boris?

                    YURI
No, I can't imagine where he has wandered off to, but I am sure he will surface when he gets hungry.

(Yuri takes a piece of cheese out of his pocket and puts it into a container.)

DMITRY
We have not heard from *Mission Control*, what time do you have?

(Yuri looks at his watch.)

YURI
It is 3.15.

DMITRY
They will contact us at 3.30 for check in...

(Dmitry looks up at Yuri's watch.)

...I have never seen you with that watch before, it is very unusual. I have never seen a triangular one before, it looks expensive.

YURI
Yes, it was very expensive, it cost my poor cousin Nikolai his life, but that is sad story.

> *(Yuri looks at his watch and then looks back at Dmitry.)*

DMITRY

What happened to your cousin Yuri?

YURI

To understand sad tale, you will need to hear it all from beginning, you better stay in your seat...

> *(Dmitry puts his green box on the floor and sits back in his chair.)*

...So, to begin. My cousin came from a poor family who lived by the river Volga in Volgograd. After coping with many illnesses as a boy and with a mother who suffered from Munchausen disease by proxy, he was forced to leave school at 15 and begin an apprenticeship at a cobblers learning how to make and repair shoes...

> *(Yuri reaches into his pocket and gets a cigarette, puts it in his mouth and lights it.)*

...One day, a man came into the shop wanting his shoes to be repaired. The shoes were different to normal shoes as they were leather and suede; they were ballroom dancing shoes. Nikolai had never seen a pair of shoes like this before and became intrigued about man who had shoes just for dancing in...

> *(Yuri takes a long puff from his cigarette and flicks the ash on the floor and takes a long stare at Dmitry.)*

...Are you alright Dmitry? You seem to be a little off colour, I hope my story is not boring you?

                    DMITRY

No, Yuri, I am just thirsty, that is all.

> *(Yuri grabs a water bottle from the side and passes it to Dmitry.)*

                    YURI

Here, drink some of this.

                    DMITRY

Thanks.

                    YURI

Where was I, ah yes. So, after the man came back for his shoes, Nikolai followed him to see where these fancy shoes, just for dancing in, were going to be worn. The man entered the town hall where they were holding a ballroom dancing competition and Nikolai followed. All night Nikolai watched the dancing and became so captivated by the gracefulness of the activity that he taught himself to dance. Nikolai practiced every night for a year and whenever he heard music, he had to dance. He went on to become one of the best dancers Russia has ever known.

DMITRY
What has this got to do with watch? So, your cousin was poor, I have several poor cousins, but they did not leave me gold watch.

YURI
I am getting to that part but first things first. He married a beautiful woman and they settled down in Moscow. For six months' everything was perfect, he danced and she watched. Then one night after a performance, a bearded ginger haired man with a strange accent entered Nikolai's dressing room. 'Where is she?' the man said. 'Who?' Nikolai replied. 'My wife, that's who.'...

(Yuri moves from his seat and starts acting out the characters.)

...'Why would I know where your wife is?' Nikolai asked. At that moment, Nikolai's wife came in, looked at the bearded man and exclaimed, 'Sandy, how did you find me?' The stranger replied, 'Never you mind lass, but you are coming home with me, we're still married in case you've forgotten.'...

> *(Yuri reaches out, grabs a small box and offers it to Dmitry.)*

...Chocolate, Dmitry? They have soft centres, very good.

                    DMITRY
Never mind chocolate, what happened next?

                    YURI
It turned out Nikolai's wife was still married to man with strange accent and ginger hair. A heated discussion followed and a fight broke out. Nikolai fell down some steps and broke his leg. His Wife leave with first husband and go back to country with strange accent.
After 3 months, Nikolai was discharged from hospital. He was never to dance again due to injury to leg. While in hospital recuperating from injury, his wife had sold their house and cleaned out his bank account, he was now broke and homeless. After living on streets for 7 years he had become a thin withdrawn creature with long hair and a beard. He had lost most of his teeth and his complexion was grey; a shell without host.

                    DMITRY
Yuri, what about watch?

                    YURI
Yes, watch. One night he had been at a

soup kitchen to get a meal. On his way out he bumped into a man playing a harmonica for loose change. The man asked him for money, but Nikolai had none. After a conversation regarding the pointlessness of begging outside a soup kitchen, they got into a fight. Nikolai was weak and could not defend himself, the man raised his right arm and plunged the harmonica into Nikolai's left lung. Although Nikolai was mortally wounded he managed to get to hospital, some 2 miles away, and collapsed on reception floor. Moments later, after they tried to resuscitate him, he died. In order to establish his identity, they searched his pockets. All they found was a picture of Nikolai and me at an awards ceremony over 10 years ago, an invitation to perform at a local music hall in two weeks time, and here is the strange thing...

(Yuri turns and looks Dmitry straight in the face.)

...In his overcoat, over 6000 Rubles in loose change. What do you make of that, Dmitry?

(At this point, Dmitry is rubbing his face and pulling at his hair.)

DMITRY

Yuri, I have listened to your story with great patience and sometimes interest, but I cannot understand what any of it has to do with your watch?

YURI

At hospital, they did not know who Nikolai was, but on back of picture he had my address and telephone number. They contacted me and that was that.

DMITRY

Yuri, watch?

YURI

Oh, yes. I went to hospital to identify Nikolai. Afterwards, they gave me picture, invitation and money. It was a nice night, so I thought I would walk home...

   (At this point Dmitry is sitting on his hands.)

...I had walked about a mile when change in pocket became quite heavy. I could see a fair over by river, flashing lights and organ music was playing, so I thought I could get rid of some coins on Kopeck Falls. I bought myself an ice cream and found a suitable machine to play. I played for an hour and lost most of it, but I could see a watch sitting on top of coins, so I kept playing. Another hour later, watch drop out from shoot...

(Yuri points at his watch.)

...This is that watch. If Nikolai had not died that night, I would not have this watch.

(Yuri begins to stare at his watch in a strange way and covers it over with his cuff.)

DMITRY
What is wrong, why are you looking at watch strangely, does it upset you Yuri?

YURI
No, it is nothing.

DMITRY
You can tell me, Yuri.

YURI
It is wrong watch, my father gave me this watch on my 21st birthday. I remember now, watch from fair stop working after 2 days and I threw in bin. That watch cost me nearly 1200 Rubles. Do Y'know, I think those machines at fair are rigged.

(Whistling and static noises are heard coming from the radio.)

VLADIMIR
This is *R.K.A Mission Control* calling *International Space Station*, over.

DMITRY
Y'know that was a good book on fly fishing and I was just starting to understand technique, but then I had to listen to your stupid story about watch. Remind me in future not to enquire about your life.

YURI
There is no need to take strop. Aren't you going to answer *Mission Control*.

DMITRY
Why don't you do it?

YURI
You are mission commander, they want to speak to train driver, not coal shovel.

(Dmitry reluctantly gets up and walks over to the radio.)

DMITRY
This is Dmitry, come in. Over.

VLADIMIR
We're getting some unusual readings coming in from all over the *Space Station*, is everything alright up there?

DMITRY
Everything is fine, a couple of relay lights have just come on, but everything else is fine...

(Dmitry presses some buttons and more lights come on.)

...Oh, wait, we are getting multiple system failures, but everything is fine. Must be a faulty reading coming from mainframe computer. I will check computer and get back to you.

                    YURI
Dmitry, here comes the American again.

                    VLADIMIR
O.K., over.

                    HANK
I am getting all kinds of system failures coming up on our computer, have you guys gotten any problems?

                    DMITRY
Just false readings that is all. We think it is problem with mainframe computer, nothing serious. Yuri and I will take a look and tell you if anything is wrong.

                    HANK
I sure hope everything is O.K., the dang T.V.'s up the spout and I can't watch the game. We were up 2 points, but anything could happen in the last 10 minutes of play. Golly, I sure hope we win.

(Yuri motions Dmitry closer.)

YURI
Dmitry, look, he has peed in his pants.

(Yuri points at Hank.)

DMITRY
My friend Yuri thinks you have peed your pants?

HANK
I guess it might look that way. I was so excited when they scored that last touchdown, I spilt my beer all over my shorts.

DMITRY
Yes, well these things do happen. Now, I must attend to computer. I will let you know when it is fixed.

HANK
O.K., well if you've got everything under control, I'll just wait in my quarters, but I get lonely without that T.V.

(Hank turns around and walks back to his quarters.)

YURI
Dmitry, is it me, or is our little American cousin a bit simple.

DMITRY

He is moron. He is embarrassment to family, so they put him in space. Imagine Yuri, a famous football player up here in *Space Station*. He doesn't even know world is flat, that's the sort of person the Space Programme are looking for these days, cowboys from Oklahoma. How could he tell anyone about Dome when all he does is watch the sports channel on T.V. I saw him just the other day watching a programme on tennis, every time the ball went off screen he looked behind T.V. to see where ball had gone. I tell you, he is a moron.

YURI

It's probably just as well he is not too bright, intelligent people ask too many questions.

DMITRY

I am going now to check mainframe computer, I will be gone quite a while, so amuse yourself and try not to break anything while I am gone.

YURI

Just one thing before you go...

DMITRY

What?

                    YURI
Where does ball go?

> *(Dmitry leaves and Yuri picks a book up from the floor and starts to read.)*

Scene fades.

ACT 3, SCENE 1

Yuri has been reading a book he found on the floor for the last 3 hours while Dmitry has been fixing the computer's mainframe. Dmitry walks into the living quarters with his green box and some mangled wires hang from underneath his arm.

                    DMITRY
What a mess, I think Boris has been at work.

    (Dmitry hands Yuri a bunch of chewed up wires.)

                    YURI
Did you see him Dmitry?

                    DMITRY
No, I did not see your mouse, just where he has been.

                    YURI
Poor Boris, I worry for his health, he must be hungry.

                    DMITRY
That mouse looked pretty fat to me, he is probably sleeping off all the plastic wiring he has been eating. You should worry more about your own health. That stupid mouse of yours nearly ruined

circuit board on main computer.

YURI
Sorry Dmitry, I will put out some peanut butter to coax him home, he loves that.

DMITRY
You have peanut butter?

YURI
Yes, but it is for Boris. If you eat it Dmitry, he will never come home. Don't worry I will save you some. Oh, did you fix T.V. for our American friend?

DMITRY
Yes, he should be watching Synchronised Swimming around about now. I imagine it was some sort of water sport. When I passed his cabin he was dressed in a bathing costume and throwing glasses of chlorinated water at himself.

YURI
As long as he is busy, it keeps him out of our hair. How did you know water was chlorinated?

DMITRY
I could smell it from corridor.

YURI
Yes, of course.

(Dmitry looks at the book Yuri is holding.)

                    DMITRY
What is that you are reading?

(Yuri looks at cover.)

                    YURI
It is called, 'Great Conspiracies of the
20th Century', by Oscar Piscine.

                    DMITRY
I wondered what had happened to that book,
I looked for it yesterday, where was it?

                    YURI
Under leg of table. Is it your book
Dmitry?

                    DMITRY
Yes, it was given to me by the author.

                    YURI
Do you know him, he seems very clever?

                    DMITRY
He is a cousin of mine on my mother's
side. He sent me book for journey.

                    YURI
I hope you don't mind me reading it?

                    DMITRY
Not at all, it is better that you read it
than use it as table leg prop.

                    YURI
Would you like a cup of tea, Dmitry?

                    DMITRY
I thought you would never ask, it is a dry
old house.

                    YURI
I will put kettle on right away...

          *(Yuri starts to light his burner
          and gets out a pan for boiling
          water.)*

...Dmitry?

                    DMITRY
Yes?

                    YURI
I was reading about assassination of KKK.
In book, the author writes that the KGB,
and SVR were involved in conspiracy to
murder president Kazimir K. Kenovsky and
that the lone gunman, known as Lee Hardly
Goodshot, was just a patty, and he could
have never pulled off job on his own.

                    DMITRY
I think you mean 'patsy', 'patty', is

piece of meat between bun surrounded with green stuff from garden and bought at Macdonald's Food Emporium. Book must have typo.

                     YURI
O.K., patsy. What mean patsy?

                    DMITRY
Y'know, erm, what is word, ah yes, he is scapegoat. He is fall guy for organisation who commit much bigger offence. Somebody has to answer for an injustice, so they use a gullible person to put blame on as a misdirection from real crime and criminals.

                     YURI
Just like when we are at your mother's house having Sunday lunch and she breaks wind something terrible, and then she calls out dog's name. Ah, tea is ready...

    (Yuri pours out the tea and hands
    a cup to Dmitry.)

...Y'know this is a fascinating book, but I was a bit confused about Lollipop moon landing in the 1960's. The author writes that moon landing was filmed in big Hollywood studio and that we did not go to moon. He said it was big hoax and it would be impossible to go through the Van Halen radiation belt as astronauts Oldsong and Armsweak had no protection against the high levels of radiation.

DMITRY
Yuri, you know we did not go to moon. Moon is beyond Dome. How could we go to moon if we cannot leave Earth.

YURI
So, we did not go to moon?

DMITRY
No. Moon is 250,000 miles away, Dome shield is 250 miles from Earth surface. We cannot pass through Dome, therefore we cannot go to moon.

YURI
When I was boy, I had action figures of astronauts Oldsong and Armsweak and model of Lunar Excursion Module. I even had moon dust. Now you say, it is lie, do Oldsong and Armsweak know?

DMITRY
I am pretty sure they do. If they don't, they will be close cousin of Hank.

(Dmitry places his cup on the table and sits back in his chair and yawns.)

DMITRY
I think I will go to bed early tonight, all of that wire replacement has made me tired.

YURI
You have worked hard this afternoon, you must be tired.

DMITRY
I am. I notice you are quite engrossed in that book?

YURI
Yes, it is fascinating stuff to the layman.

DMITRY
Yes, very. Is the print big enough for you?

YURI
Not bad. The font and kernelling are both good.

DMITRY
I was just wondering how you can read book, but cannot see to help me fix elliptical card?

YURI
Did I not tell you. I found my contact lenses between two packets of sausages.

DMITRY
Well that is good, you can help me from now on.

YURI
I was not concealing the fact that I had found my *contacts*, it just slipped my mind.

DMITRY
No matter, we have plenty days left on *Space Station*.

(Yuri, goes over to a locker and takes out some brandy.)

YURI
Would you like a spot of brandy in your tea, Dmitry?

DMITRY
What brandy?

YURI
Here. I brought it along for cooking, but a little dash in the bottom of your cup will help you sleep.

DMITRY
'Just a Wee Drap', as your Scottish cousins would say...

    (Yuri adds some brandy to Dmitry's cup.)

...Speaking of Scottish cousins, I was thinking about your watch story, not the watch part, but the injustice precipitated by Nikolai's wife. Her running off back to her first husband and taking all his money.

YURI
Yes, it is a sad tale, but I did not tell you everything.

DMITRY
I am tired Yuri, at this moment I am afraid to ask...

    (Dmitry drinks his brandy.)

...What else is there to tell?

YURI
When Nikolai's wife goes to leave Russia with ginger haired man, she is stopped at the airport by Customs. She did not declare on form that she had over 600,000 Rubles, so Customs confiscated it.

DMITRY
How much money did she have?

YURI
Her bag and pockets were full, her suitcases were full, even ginger haired man carried some in his sporran. They were carrying over 50 million Rubles between them.

DMITRY
50 Million Rubles, that's a lot of Cabbage. What happened next?

YURI
They were forced to leave without money. On way back to land where they wear skirt and squeeze bag on hilltop, their boat sank.

DMITRY
Boat! What boat? You said they were at airport!

YURI
Ginger haired man had outstanding warrant for arrest and at airport they had to make a break for it. They managed to escape and climbed aboard a cattle boat. They waited on board through the night to avoid detection, but boat left before they could get off. Two days later, boat gets caught in storm and sinks. No survivors.

DMITRY
I would like to say I feel sorry for them, but I don't. What happened to money?

YURI
As with all money that is taken at airport, it is seized by government until a legal claim is made for it by parties concerned. Nikolai did not know of his wife's fate or the money he could have claimed back.

DMITRY
How do you know about it, Yuri?

YURI
Because I have money.

DMITRY
You have money?

YURI
Yes.

DMITRY
How did that come about?

YURI
When Nikolai die, it was in newspaper and I was mentioned as being his cousin and being present at the hospital the night of his death. Nikolai's solicitor had been looking for him for years, but he never showed up on radar. When solicitor saw

article in paper about Nikolai's death, he contacted me and we started legal proceedings to get money back. I got everything, minus 10% legal fees.

DMITRY
What have you done with money Yuri?

YURI
I have bought various food chains and supermarkets, invested in overseas business ventures, bought stocks and shares and have a very nice property portfolio in Moscow. The rest is in bank making interest.

DMITRY
You are full of surprises, Yuri. I never know what you will say or do. Well, I must get some rest, I need a good sleep.

(Dmitry rises from his chair and disappears behind the curtain.)

Scene fades.

ACT 3, SCENE 2

It is the next morning and Yuri is washing some pans and plates in a bowl. Dmitry walks in from behind the curtain, he has just woken up and looks tired and dishevelled.

DMITRY
What time did you get up?

YURI
It was early, I had a restless night thinking about poor Boris, so I had to go and look for him.

DMITRY
Did you see any signs of mouse chewing?

YURI
No, I can't understand it, he has never stayed away this long before.

DMITRY
Did you see any signs of our American friend?

YURI
Yes. I walked past his cabin at 5am this morning and he was dressed in a black cape and a blindfold.

DMITRY
What was he doing?

YURI
I could not see at first, so I went to have a closer look. He had a tail in his right hand and he was trying to pin it on the backside of donkey picture on wall. He spun around 6 times and then lunged to the wall, knocking over a lamp and some Matchbox cars. He then shouted out, 'I am so disoriented'. What does this word mean Dmitry?

DMITRY
It is racial slur, it means that you have a dislike for people and things from the East.

YURI
Funny, I wouldn't have thought his brain was that developed to think that way.

(Outside, in the corridor, footsteps are heard approaching their quarters. A man's voice is heard, and then, a thin scrawny looking guy with slicked back hair enters.)

GEORGE LONDON
I think he meant to say, 'disorientated', in other words -'Dizzy'. Sorry to butt in...

(George holds out his hand to Yuri.)

...I'm George London, one of the English astronauts on board. I meant to pop over a couple of days ago, but we've been having a bit of a Scrabble competition for food coupons. Do either of you play Scrabble?

DMITRY
No, we're too busy for silliness, and English food coupon has no worth in Russia.

GEORGE LONDON
Oh, I see...

(Yuri pulls out a packet of cigarettes and takes one, lights it and sits down.)

...Well, I just popped over to say hello and to see if you had any spare *ciggys*. I could smell the sweet aroma of tailor-made Camel cigarettes wafting from your quarters and I could resist the temptation to come over and meet you chaps no longer. I have some rich tea biscuits to trade?

(Dmitry looks over to Yuri and shakes his head.)

YURI
I am sorry, I only have enough for myself,

there is a good chance I will run out before our little space trek ends, so I cannot trade.

                GEORGE LONDON
Well, O.K. If you ever fancy a game of Scrabble, new games start every night at 8pm. It was nice talking to you. Bye.

                DMITRY
Nice talking to you too...

    (George leaves and Dmitry turns to Yuri.)

...See, what did I tell you. We have not even seen the English. The minute they need something, they are on the scrounge.

                YURI
He seemed pleasant enough, but slightly greasy for my tastes.

                DMITRY
The English are not to be trusted, Yuri. They carry flag around, put in ground and make a home. Even in war, it is all about cups of tea and pushing wooden tanks and planes around on big map. Then it is off home for cigars and port. I don't even like smell, did you smell him Yuri?

YURI
That's why I lit cigarette, his cheap cologne was offensive to my olfactory system. But his shoes, his shoes were awful - a lace-less brogue.

DMITRY
We will keep our distance Yuri, but be polite if we see him.

YURI
I think that is best plan.

DMITRY
Why couldn't we have been on board with the Chinese. They always have good food. The stuff that comes out of a Wok is just heaven, I love Russian food, but secretly Yuri, my heart belongs to China.

YURI
Me too. King Prawn Chow Mein, Beef Hoisin, Sweet & Sour Pork Balls, Chicken and Mushroom, Wonton soup, Special Fried Rice, Ginger with Spring Onions... the list of goodies goes on and on.

DMITRY
I don't suppose you brought a Wok with you?

YURI
I am afraid not, Dmitry. But we will have special treat when we get home. I will

even pay for it.

DMITRY
That is very kind of you, Yuri.

YURI
Now, shall I make breakfast?

DMITRY
Yes, what are we having?

YURI
Porridge, bacon and eggs, fresh coffee and croissants.

DMITRY
Good. I will set table.

(Dmitry starts to lay the table with condiments, cutlery and plates. Yuri takes out his burner, cafetière and some pans to start cooking.)

YURI
Does Chinese military have good ration pack Yuri?

DMITRY
Yes, I believe they have very good dry products: Lotus root, noodles, rice, chicken, duck, vegetables, soups, prawn crackers with lots of pouches of ginger,

five spice, soy sauce, oyster sauce, dried garlic and chillies.

YURI
It must be a joy to be in Chinese army, but I would not like to be in battle.

DMITRY
Why is that?

YURI
Enemy would hear you from miles away.

DMITRY
What do you mean?

YURI
When army march, it must sound like dairy cow with bell. Just imagine it, everyone has wok, kitchen utensils and gas burner. It must make dreadful racket when they walk.

DMITRY
Perhaps Wok is worn on head as helmet.

YURI
That must be it, I am sure that's the answer.

(Crackling and whistling is heard from the radio.)

VLADIMIR
This is *R.K.A Mission Control* calling *International Space Station*. Come in, over.

DMITRY
What now? Why are they calling at this time? This is just annoying, this is just like nuisance call you get at home. You are just about to sit down for a meal and phone rings, *'Hello Mr Usakov, the government are funding windows for poorly insulated houses in your area, do you own your own home?'* I can't stand that, if you are polite, they keep talking, if you hang up, they phone back and say we were disconnected, you can't win.

VLADIMIR
This is *R.K.A Mission Control* calling *International Space Station*. Come in, over.

(Dmitry walks over to the radio.)

DMITRY
Yes, yes, what is it?

VLADIMIR
Who is this?

DMITRY
It is Dmitry, who did you expect?

VLADIMIR
Do you usually speak to a superior officer in such a tone?

(Dmitry starts to turn the dial on the radio.)

DMITRY
Sorry, we are losing you, say again?...

(Dmitry turns the radio off.)

...O.K., Yuri, let's eat.

YURI
Dmitry, what are you doing? He will be mad when you talk to him later.

(Yuri lays out the food on the table and they begin to eat.)

DMITRY
Who cares? Stupid little turnip thief.

YURI
What are you saying Dmitry?

DMITRY
That Vladimir. He and his father used to steal turnips from my uncle's farm when I

was a boy. They would creep out on to field when moon was high in sky and they would steal turnips and sell at local market. My uncle lost his farm because of people like that Vladimir. When I first started in Space Programme, he could not even look me in the eye, now he thinks he is big shot.

                    YURI
He must have stolen a lot of turnips from your uncle's farm to put him out of business?

                    DMITRY
You have no idea, Yuri. It is criminal what people can get away with, and my poor uncle, scraping a living together selling flotation tanks to the army.

                    YURI
Flotation Tanks?

                    DMITRY
Y'know, torture chamber. Ice cold water in steel tank and in total darkness.

                    YURI
Could your uncle not do something else?

                    DMITRY
Like what? He is farmer, he can barely spell his own name. Planting cabbages and turnips was his trade, he only has this

job because nobody else wants it. No, he is destined to live out his life in sales.

                    YURI
Could you not put in a good word for him at headquarters?

                    DMITRY
Yuri, are you mad? How do you think he got job?...

    (Dmitry finishes off his food,
    grabs his green box and heads for
    the corridor.)

...Thanks for that, Yuri. A real treat. I am going to check on computer, so when we speak to H.Q., I can report everything is perfect.

                    YURI
O.K., I will wash up this stuff and see you in a while... But before you go, I have been meaning to ask, why do you always carry green box under arm?

                    DMITRY
It is family heirloom, it's very precious to me.

(Dmitry holds the box up and looks at it.)

                    YURI
I noticed other day some fishing flies peeping out from top of compartment, what's so precious about that?

    (Yuri taps a cigarette on the table.)

If you had been left gold bar by relatives, I might see need to covet case, but old fishing tackle is worthless. It is even more worthless in space, there is no river or fish!

    (Yuri lights his cigarette and Dmitry looks on at his box with great pride.)

                    DMITRY
My great, great, great, great grandfather gave this box to his son, and he in turn gave it to his son and so on...

                    YURI
...And now you have it?

                    DMITRY
Yes, that is right.

YURI
But why is it important?

DMITRY
In 1891, in Volga river, one of biggest sturgeon in world was caught using tackle in green box. It produced enough caviar to fill a million cans. It made my family's wealth. Green box is everything I am, it is my heritage.

YURI
But why have it here?

DMITRY
My wife does not like colour green, she says she will throw old box of fish tales in river where it belongs. Olga ask, 'Where is money? In 1891 a million cans would be fortune, where fortune?' I tell her, generation before me lose money on horse track. Then she wants to know how person can drop fortune on ground and not see it. I try to tell her money is not everything, but she says that I do not have to queue for lemons at store and row starts. No, box is safe here. Now, I must be going.

Scene fades.

ACT 3, SCENE 3

Four hours have passed and the cabin looks spick and span. Yuri is reading his book and Dmitry comes into the cabin with his green box under his arm. His demeanour has much improved and he seems quite happy.

>   DMITRY
> Yuri?
>
>   YURI
> What is it, Dmitry?
>
>   DMITRY
> I have found Boris.
>
>   YURI
> Is he alive, Dmitry?
>
>   DMITRY
> He, or should I say she, is doing very well. Perhaps Doris would be a better name.
>
>   YURI
> She?
>
>   DMITRY
> Yes. You are also a grandfather!

YURI

The man in pet shop sell mouse as a 'He' for premium rate. Just wait until we get back home. Where is Boris?

DMITRY

Doris, has had a litter of five babies and has been hiding out in emergency escape pod in dry food container.

YURI

That is why I could not find him, I mean her. I did not look in escape pod. I will go to see now...

(Just as Yuri is about to leave the cabin an explosion is heard, the Space Station starts to move around violently and an alarm sounds repeatedly. Debris from the Space Station is seen floating past their window.)

...What is that Dmitry?

DMITRY

Mainframe computer has exploded, the whole place will go up. We only have about 20 minutes before *Station* is consumed by fire.

YURI

What shall we do, Dmitry?

DMITRY
Quickly Yuri, to the escape pod.

(Dmitry and Yuri start to make their way to the escape pod, when the English astronauts are seen climbing in. A few seconds later, the pod launches.)

YURI
What will we do now?

DMITRY
Quickly, back to cabin and put on space suit. We are better off outside when this thing blows up.

YURI
I agree. What about Hank?

DMITRY
I will get him. Go put your suit on.

(Yuri returns to his cabin to put his space suit on. The Space Station begins to rock violently and gas pockets start erupting everywhere. Dmitry returns shortly without Hank.)

YURI
Where is Hank?

DMITRY
He is dead.

YURI
Dead. How?

DMITRY
I didn't know at first, but it looks like he swallowed his tongue.

YURI
Swallowed his tongue?

DMITRY
Yes. On table I could see a book - 'Teach yourself how to yodel'. Looks like he got technique wrong and swallowed his tongue.

(More debris floats past the window and the Space Station starts to shake and make noises.)

YURI
Oh, well, I don't think we have time to mourn. Let's get out of here.

(Dmitry and Yuri make their way to the airlock to get out of the Space Station. Outside, they use their jetpacks to drift away to a safe distance. They look back and the Space Station starts to come apart. Another explosion happens and a fire breaks out.)

DMITRY

That was close, Yuri. We were nearly fried chicken.

YURI

I am glad we are alive, but how long can we live in space suit?

DMITRY

A few hours.

(Dmitry takes his green box from under his arm and opens it.)

YURI

What is really in box? Don't tell me stupid story about fish, you are like Gollum with ring...

(Dmitry opens the box and pulls out a bottle of vodka.)

...Vodka? Now I understand why your mood changes. You are grumpy old man, then you disappear with box and when you return,

you are happy, like child with ice cream.
It all makes sense, but I don't see how it
will help us out here?

                    DMITRY
Yuri, it is always a good idea to have a
bottle of vodka, even if outlook is poor.

                    YURI
But what are we going to do, Dmitry?

        *(Dmitry looks over at the broken
        Space Station and smiles.)*

                    DMITRY
Don't worry, I will think of something.

                    YURI
At least Doris and her little ones will go
home. It is good to be grandparent.

                    DMITRY
You and that mouse. It is because of
mouse we are in this mess.

                    YURI
We don't know if mouse cause explosion,
the English certainly made their feet
their best friends when big bang happened.
They didn't even care about us, they just
left.

                    DMITRY
Maybe you are right. It is strange that

Hank would swallow his tongue. Yuri, we are victim in big cover up. Let's get back to *Station*, I think some of it is still in good shape and our quarters look practically untouched. There may be a way out of this thing yet.

YURI
Do you think we are your mother's dog?

DMITRY
Only if we roll over and do nothing. C'mon Yuri, we shall bite my mother's hand.

(Yuri and Dmitry head back towards the Space Station to inspect the damage. As they approach, debris falls from the Space Station and fires break out throughout the ship. Below, the Earth continues to spin and the clouds roll by without a care.)

YURI
Looks pretty bad from here Dmitry.

DMITRY
Yes, those fires are looking quite serious.

                    YURI
          What are we going to do?

                    DMITRY
          Let me think a minute.

Scene fades.

                 To be continued...

The fun continues and the adventure begins in:

          'Beyond the Dome'

Printed in Poland
by Amazon Fulfillment
Poland Sp. z o.o., Wrocław